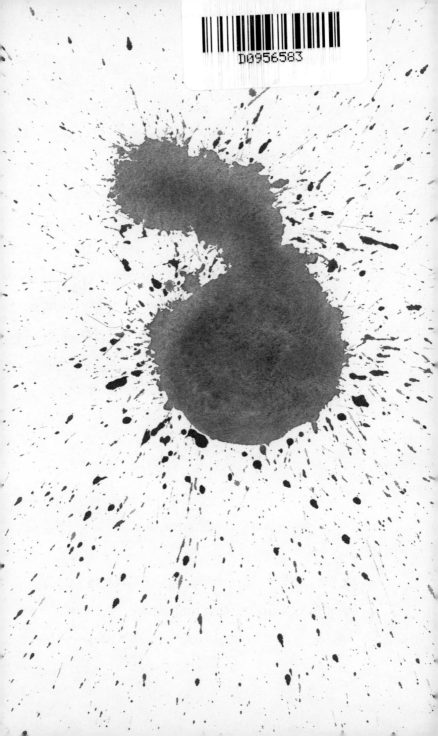

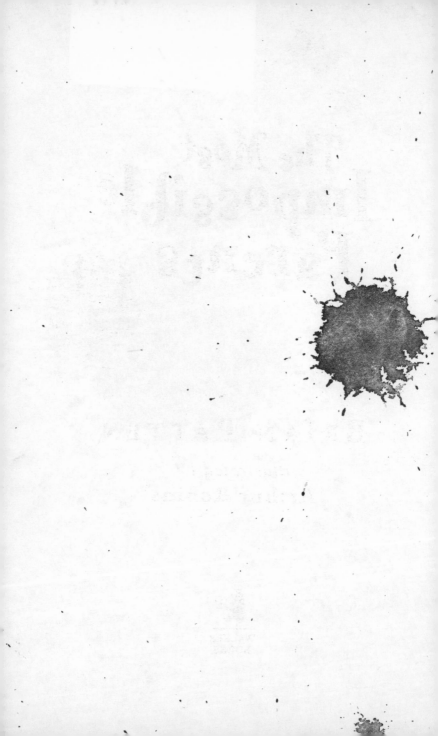

The Most Impossible Parents

BRIAN PATTEN

illustrated by
Arthur Robins

WALKER
BOOKS

For impossible parents everywhere
B.P.

For Sav and Nicola
with love from Grandad
A.R.

This edition first published 2010 by Walker Books Ltd
87 Vauxhall Walk, London SE11 5HJ

2 4 6 8 10 9 7 5 3 1

Text © 1994, 2000, 2010 Brian Patten
Illustrations © 1994, 2000, 2010 Arthur Robins

The right of Brian Patten and Arthur Robins to be identified as
author and illustrator respectively of this work has been asserted by
them in accordance with the Copyright, Designs and Patents Act 1988

This book has been typeset in StempelSchneidler

Printed in Great Britain by Clays Ltd, St Ives plc

British Library Cataloguing in Publication Data:
a catalogue record for this book is available from the British Library

ISBN 978-1-4063-2186-9

www.walker.co.uk

Contents

Parents' Day
7

Mr Norm the Poet
33

The Impossible Parents
Go Green
59

Parents' Day

Ben and Mary Norm thought their mum and dad were the best parents in the world. The trouble was, they also thought they were the most embarrassing parents in the world. Mr and Mrs Norm were always doing stuff other parents would never dream of doing, and they had no idea how awful they looked.

For example, Dad had a grotty grey ponytail that Ben and Mary hated. It was gruesome. It dangled from the back of his head and looked disgusting. Mary always said that if someone shook it, they'd get enough dandruff to fill a talcum powder tin. Dad also had a ring in the corner of his right nostril. The trouble was, it was rusty because every time he had a cold his nose dripped and the ring got wet.

"Ponytails belong on ponies, not adults," said Ben.

"And rings belong in bulls' noses, not in grown-ups' nostrils," replied Mary. "If it rusts any more he'll get some dreadful farmyard disease, then he'll have to be put down."

That wasn't the worst of it. Not only did their dad have a ring through his nose and a ponytail, he also wore a puce-coloured bobble hat and a black string vest.

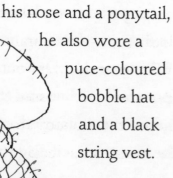

"Can you think of anyone who looks worse than Dad?" moaned Ben.

"Yes," said Mary, "I can."

Mary meant her mum.

Mrs Norm often wore a fishnet body stocking as part of her ordinary wardrobe but, as if that wasn't bad enough, you should have seen how she dressed for work.

Unfortunately for her children, Mrs Norm was a belly-dancer and she was employed part-time by the local Turkish restaurant. Whenever she went out to work, Ben and Mary crossed their fingers and hoped that nobody from their school would be going to the restaurant with their parents.

It would be awful if they saw Mrs Norm wobbling her vast belly and shaking her tassels to the sound of Turkish bagpipe music. Ben and Mary took a little comfort from the fact that part of their mum's outfit was a veil. They hoped that as long as she kept the veil on, no one would recognize her.

It wasn't only the way their mum and dad looked that embarrassed Mary and Ben. It was also Mr and Mrs Norm's manners, and their attitude to life. Mr and Mrs Norm didn't care one hoot what other people thought of them. Dad would pick his nose and flick bogies at flies. Mum would practise belly-dancing in front of the window or take her shoes off and paint her toenails, which doesn't sound so bad – until you've smelled her feet. Every time she took her shoes off, the cat fainted.

It was Mary's least favourite person, Alice Frimp, who started all the children at school boasting about their parents. One day they were standing around in the playground when Alice Frimp said, "My mum's responsible for keeping the Queen's clothes looking fresh. She's a royal fashion consultant."

"Well, my dad's a test pilot," said Charlie Buggins.

"My mum's a high-powered businesswoman who used to be a brain surgeon," boasted Mavis Mayhem.

"Mine's an opera singer," said Pattie Rotti.

Mary nearly told the truth. She nearly said her mum was a belly-dancer.

"Mine's a b-be-bel-ballet dancer!" she said instead.

"And Dad's a fire-fighter," said Ben.

12

Mary thought Alice Frimp was a real grub.
That very same day their teacher, Miss
Jones, said, "Don't forget, it's Parents' Day
next Friday. I'm looking forward to meeting
all your parents for the first time."

"I couldn't stand Alice Frimp or any of her horrible gang seeing Mum and Dad. They'll poke fun at us for ever," wailed Mary as they walked home after school.

Ben felt the same. He wished he hadn't said their dad was a fire-fighter. You don't see many string-vested fire-fighters in puce-coloured bobble hats who have ponytails and wear rings in their noses.

What if Dad absent-mindedly flicked a bogey at Miss Jones? It was the kind of thing he might do. And then he'd pick something from between his teeth – with the same finger!

Ben and Mary were mortified. Miss Jones would be friendly to their parents, and pretend not to notice their habits. But what would she really think, deep down inside? There must be something they could do to stop the Dreaded Parents coming along to Parents' Day.

"It's simple." said Ben. "We just won't tell them about it."

"Right," said Mary, "we'll keep Parents' Day a secret."

But their mum and dad already knew.

Every single parent had received a letter from Miss Jones.

"I can't wait to come along to Parents' Day," said Dad.

"Neither can I," said Mum. "I'll wear my leather jacket – the one with the slashes – and my fishnet body stocking. You'll be proud of us."

That night Ben and Mary held a powwow
in their bedroom. The first thing they decided
to do was to tackle the problem of Dad.

At midnight, when Mr and Mrs Norm
were snoring loudly, Ben and Mary tiptoed
into their parents' bedroom. Mary had a
pair of very sharp scissors. With a few quick
hacks, off came Dad's disgusting ponytail.

That was one less thing for Alice Frimp to be snide about. Ben had found a pair of bolt cutters in the garage. With a few expert snips, off came Dad's rusty nose-ring. Next they took a pile of his tatty string vests and greasy bobble hats from the cupboard and put them in the dustbin. That was enough for one night.

When they went down to breakfast
next morning, Mr Norm was sitting in the
kitchen. He was completely bald except for
a bit of stubble, and Mrs Norm was busy
drawing something on his
head. She was using an
old-fashioned pen-nib
dipped in red and
black ink. When she'd
finished, Mary and
Ben saw what Mum
had drawn. It was a
large spider's web with
a big fat spider sitting
in the middle of it.

"For some mysterious
reason I started losing my hair last night,"
said Mr Norm, "so me and Mum decided to
shave it all off and use my head as a canvas."

"We're just trying out a few design ideas,"
said Mrs Norm. "If we like this one we'll get

a tattooist to do it in permanent ink."

"But Dad can't have a spider's web tattooed on his head!" cried Ben.

"Of course he can," said Mrs Norm. "It's not illegal, dear."

There was no answer to that.

When Mum had finished, Mary came up close and studied Dad's head properly. No matter what else she thought, Mary had to admit that her mum was a pretty good artist. She had drawn a very realistic fly caught in the centre of the web. Not only that, the fly was half eaten by the spider.

Ben moaned. Mary moaned. The spider's web was even worse than the ponytail. And there were only a few days left before Parents' Day! They were frantic! Why did they have such impossible parents?

"If Mum and Dad were a bit more intelligent, then they'd know we don't want them coming into school!" said Ben.

"The cat's more intelligent than them," snorted Mary.

"I know that already," said Ben, who thought Smudge the cat was the best cat in the world. "Have you seen the way he studies the fridge when Mum opens it?"

Mary said she had.

"Well," said Ben, "yesterday Smudge brought a dead mouse in from the garden and dropped it by the fridge door."

"So?"

"So a few moments later Dad comes in from the pub and puts the mouse in the fridge. He thought it must have dropped out."

Mary sighed.

Dad was Dad. She loved him the way he was even if the way he was wasn't the way she wanted him to be.

It was every kid's dilemma.

At school nobody seemed very enthusiastic about Parents' Day. In fact, everybody looked extemely worried. Even Mary's arch-enemy, Alice Frimp, who had started them all boasting about their parents, seemed worried.

"I don't think my mum will be coming to Parents' Day after all," she said.

"I hope … er, I mean, I think mine will be too busy as well," said Pattie Rotti.

When Charlie Buggins said that he was looking forward to meeting Ben's dad because he was a real fire-fighter, Ben blushed and felt very hot. He wished he hadn't told a fib. And Mary nearly burst into tears.

Alice Frimp was a double grub, getting them all boasting about what their parents did!

Mary thought of the horrible humiliation she would feel if it was discovered that her mum was a belly-dancer instead of a ballet dancer.

And there was only one day to go!

That night Ben and Mary sneaked back into their parents' bedroom. This time they worked on Mum.

They found her wild blue glitter-wig and
hid it behind the wardrobe, along with her
snakeskin belt and her alligator-skin shoes.

Next they rummaged about in the
cupboard.

They found her fishnet body stocking,
which they stuffed into a bin-bag along
with her pink feather boa and
belly-dancing outfit. They
also found more of Mr
Norm's bobble hats
and tatty old vests and
threw these in as well.
Then they took the
whole lot downstairs and
dumped it in the dustbin.

Next morning, when they went down to
breakfast, there was a police officer standing
in the kitchen talking to Mr and Mrs Norm,
who were both wrapped in towels.

"A wild blue glitter-wig and a fishnet body stocking, you say, madam? And a nose-ring, you say, sir? Stolen from your bedroom?"

"Yes, it seems there's been a burglar prowling around. He's obviously got good taste," said Mr Norm.

"It means I'll have nothing to wear for Parents' Day today!" wailed Mrs Norm.

"Ah, Parents' Day. That might explain a few things," said the police officer thoughtfully.

He turned to Mary and Ben. "Are you two *quite* sure you don't know anything about this?" he asked.

Ben and Mary blushed bright red. Sweat trickled down their sides.

"It's just that we often get mysterious goings-on just before Parents' Day," the police officer said. "Well, if I see a burglar wearing a glitter-wig, a nose-ring and a belly-dancer's outfit I'll let your mum and dad know immediately."

The police officer put his notebook away and left. Ben and Mary could have sworn he winked at them as he went out the door.

After Mary and Ben recovered from the shock of seeing a police officer in the house, they were quite pleased with themselves. Their parents had nothing much to wear now except towels, and they couldn't very well go to Parents' Day wrapped in towels. Ben and Mary left for school that morning with light hearts.

At school everyone looked happy again. Compared with how miserable they'd appeared after the announcement of Parents' Day, they positively glowed.

In fact, everyone looked a bit too pleased with themselves. They'd all been up to something, Mary was sure – but what? Could they possibly have been trying to stop *their* parents from coming along to Parents' Day too? Surely not. Surely nobody else had such impossible parents – or did they?

"Quiet, now!" said Miss Jones. "You all know it's Parents' Day, so I want you to be on your best behaviour."

She looked at her watch. "They're coming soon," she said. Miss Jones seemed to know exactly what the children were thinking. She seemed to know exactly what was going to happen.

It was about twenty minutes before the parents arrived…

The children looked out of the windows.

Fifteen minutes…

Then ten minutes … nine … eight … seven … six … five … four … three … two … then—

The classroom door burst open and Alice Frimp's mum rushed in. Everyone could tell by the uniform she wore that she worked in the dry cleaner's around the corner from Buckingham Palace. So much for her being the Queen's fashion consultant! Alice Frimp had fibbed!

But then
so had Pattie
Rotti. Her
mum wasn't
an opera
singer – she was
a traffic warden.
And Charlie
Buggins's dad
wasn't a test
pilot. He drove
the wet-fish
lorry. You could
tell by the smell.

The parents piled in, one after the other.

Everybody thought everyone else's
parents were amazing and wonderful and
that only their own parents were impossible.

"It always happens like this," said Miss
Jones. "All children think there is something
embarrassing about their own parents."

Then, last of all, Ben and Mary's parents stormed in. They had taken their clothes out of the dustbin. Mrs Norm wore her belly-dancing costume and everyone thought she was the most amazing mum ever.

Miss Jones was very impressed. She'd always had a secret desire to be a belly-dancer, so Mrs Norm showed her how to do it. She stood up on a desk and did a fantastic dance. Then Miss Jones tried. She was a natural. "I'm giving up teaching this afternoon and becoming a belly-dancer instead!" she shouted.

The head teacher thought Miss Jones should have set a better example and not tried belly-dancing in front of the class, but everyone agreed that the head was just jealous.

As for Miss Jones, she never did give up her job and become a belly-dancer, but everyone had a really fabulous Parents' Day.

In fact, it was the most wonderful Parents' Day there had ever been.

Mr Norm the Poet

After Parents' Day things returned to normal
for a while. Mr Norm was sitting at the
kitchen table picking his nose and staring
into space, and Mrs Norm was sitting across
from him reading a newspaper and sewing
tassels to her belly-dancing outfit.

"I'm bored," sighed Mr Norm. "Bored,
bored, bored. I want to do something totally
different."

"Of course, dear. But what?" asked Mrs
Norm.

"I don't know yet. Something easy," he said. "How about becoming a poet?" suggested Mrs Norm. "You often sit staring into mid-air, doing absolutely nothing. And if you're a poet, that's part of the job. You could start by entering this poetry competition."

Mrs Norm pushed her newspaper across the table.

Dad thought Mrs Norm's idea was a rather good one. It was true, he did like staring into space. He was pretty good at it and sometimes did it for hours.

Ben and Mary thought the idea of Dad writing a poem was daft.

"Dad can hardly write his name, never mind poetry!" said Mary.

"Of course I can," said Mr Norm. "It's easy. The hardest thing will be filling in the entry form."

"What kind of poem does it have to be?" asked Ben.

Mr Norm licked his biro, getting ink on his tongue. "It says on the entry form that it has to be a soothing nursery-rhyme kind of poem. The winning entry is going to be printed on a greetings card."

"But how can you write a poem when you don't like writing?" asked Ben.

"You don't even like reading," said Mary. "You only ever read to us once when we were little."

"That's right," remembered Ben. "And even then we had to help *you* out with some of the words."

Mr Norm said they were talking a load of nonsense, which they weren't. He put his head down and began scribbling in order to avoid listening to them.

After half an hour Dad slapped his pencil down on the table.

"I've finished!" he shouted. "Listen to this:

Have you ever seen a hairy fairy?
I know one.
Her name is Mary."

"You're not entering that!" exclaimed Mary.

"Certainly not," agreed Mum. "Your daughter is neither hairy nor a fairy."

Mr Norm looked crestfallen that no one seemed to like his efforts. He bent back down over his paper.

"I'll try again," he sighed.

But nothing happened. Not a single word occurred to him. His mind was a perfect blank.

"This is going to be harder than I thought," he said.

"Just stare vacantly into space a bit longer, dear," said Mrs Norm encouragingly. "I'm sure an idea will pop into your head sooner or later."

And she was right. After staring into space for ages, Dad gave a little shout. "What rhymes with 'chop off your head'?" he asked.

"'Under the bed,'" answered Ben. "But you can't have people chopping off heads in soothing nursery rhymes. Don't forget, the poetry competition judges want poems that can go on greetings cards."

But Mr Norm wasn't listening. He always thought he knew best, even though he never did. He scribbled down Ben's suggestion – "under the bed".

Next he asked Mary what rhymed with "crime" and she said, "time".

After that he asked Mrs Norm what rhymed with "crawling about" and she said, "You'd better look out".

Then he turned to Ben again and asked what rhymed with "hook" and Ben said "book".

This went on for over an hour.
Everybody was fed up with Dad asking for
rhymes and so they left him sitting at the
kitchen table, shouting out words that were
totally unsuitable for any kind of greetings
card whatsoever.

When Mr Norm finished writing the
poem – which took a long time – he put it
in an envelope, along with the entry form,
and posted it to the Poetry Competition
without showing it to anyone. Then he took
out his new nose ring and polished it, which
he always did when he was worried about
things.

What he was worrying about mostly was his poem. Should he have written "withered hand" or "wizened hand" in the first verse? And in the same verse should he have mentioned green gunge pouring out of a goblin's nose or should he have made it yellow gunge? He fretted about this for weeks. And then, finally, a letter arrived from the Poetry Judges.

"Dear Mr Snorm…" it began.

"Snorm! They've gone and spelled my name wrong," he said indignantly. "Snorm! Whoever heard of a poet called Snorm!"

"Never mind, dear," said Mrs Norm, "let's hear what the rest of the letter says."

"It says, 'Thank you for your wonderful

poem. You've won first prize
in the poetry competition.'"

Mary was dumbfounded.
Ben was flabbergasted. The
cat twitched. Even Mrs Norm
was a little bit astonished.

The idea of Dad winning anything was
highly unusual.

"Are you *sure* the letter's not meant for
someone else?" asked Ben.

"Of course not," said Mr Norm, still
indignant. "They've simply spelled my name
wrong."

Mrs Norm agreed. "Poetry Judges are
notoriously bad at spelling poets' names,"
she said. "After all, whoever heard of a poet
called Snorm?"

"And whoever heard of one called Norm?"
said Mary. "Can I see a copy of the poem?"
She found it impossible to believe that Dad
had won the competition.

Mr Norm drew a crumpled piece of paper from his pocket. He smoothed it out and handed it to her.

Mary tried to read it but she couldn't. She showed it to Ben. He tried to read it, but he couldn't either. The writing was a series of smudges and squiggles and crossings-out that only Mr Norm understood.

The only bit Mary could make out was a few lines at the end of the first verse. She read them out loud:

"There's a withered old hand crawling about,
And a horrible goblin with green gunge

pouring out
Of its nose—"

She stopped reading and looked at Dad in disbelief. "This doesn't sound like a prize-winning poem to me," she said.

Ben said he thought it sounded cool, but that he could understand why the poetry judges might not like it.

When she heard the bit about green gunge, even Mrs Norm had a spot of difficulty accepting that Dad had won the competition. "The idea was to write a sweet nursery rhyme for a greetings card, dear," she reminded him. "Do you think perhaps you've been a little over-enthusiastic with the withered hand?"

"If I found a hand crawling about under the bed, I wouldn't be at all enthusiastic," said Mary. "I'd be terrified."

"Pah! All you'd have to do is stamp on it," said Mr Norm. "It's what any sensible child would do. Why, if I'd found a withered hand crawling about under the bed when I was little I'd have bashed it with the alarm clock."

Mr Norm decided everyone was jealous that he'd won the competition. "It is obvious they thought that my poem was a work of genius," he declared. "Anyway, the prize-giving's next week and we're all going to it."

And that was that.

It was lovely and sunny on the day of the prize-giving. Everybody was up early. Birds sang and the sky was as blue as a peacock's tail. Mrs Norm spent hours getting ready. She painted her toenails, put on a pair of false eyelashes and struggled into her plastic miniskirt.

Mr Norm also dressed up for the occasion. He wore a bright blue suit that had once belonged to his granddad. It had some egg stains on it and was a bit worn out on the behind, but Mr Norm thought it was the best suit ever. It had tight trousers and a black velvet collar. The only snag was that it smelled of mothballs, even after he'd sprayed it with air freshener from the bathroom and sprinkled the pockets with talcum powder.

The prize-giving was being held in the Town Hall. Mr and Mrs Norm decided to walk there, which Ben and Mary hated. It wasn't that they disliked walking.

It was just that walking with their parents
when they were dressed up was the most
embarrassing thing in the world.

They lagged as far behind as possible.

"Do you think that Dad can really have
won?" asked Ben.

"Of course not," said Mary.

Because Dad was holding the map upside
down, they were late arriving at the town
hall. There were forty people in the hall,
and on the stage three judges sat at a long
table. The main judge was a large round lady
in a green hat. When the Norms took their
seats she was introducing a man from the

greetings card company, whose job it was to thank everyone for coming along.

He twittered on about all the wonderful poems that had been entered into the competition. He said there had been dozens about butterflies and flowers. He never mentioned goblins or gunge, which made Ben think maybe Mary was right about Dad not winning.

It was time for the prize-giving. The lady in the green hat introduced the prize-winners in reverse order. Mr Norm itched with impatience. He could hardly breathe, he was so excited.

The lady in the green hat said, "Third prize goes to Mr Dirge for his poem about honey-bees blowing in the wind."

Mr Dirge came up onto the stage and read his poem. It was awful.

Next came the winner of the second prize, a lady called Mrs Piddle, who read a poem about ducks that began:

"Oh, what luck
To be a duck
With feathers no one
Wants to pluck."

It was not quite as bad as the first poem but Mr and Mrs Norm were a bit confused.

48

They couldn't understand why nobody wanted to pluck the duck's feathers. Mr Norm whispered that maybe the duck was too thin, or inedible.

Then the big moment came. "And now for the winner of the competition to find the best poem to go on a greetings card," said the lady in the green hat. "The winner is … "

Mr Norm was down the aisle like greased lightening.

He was halfway up the steps onto the stage before he heard the judge say, "Mr Snorm."

"I'm Mr Norm – not Mr Snorm!" he declared angrily.

And someone close behind him said,
"And I'm Mr Snorm – not Mr Norm!"

Mr Norm and Mr Snorm stood on the
stage glaring at each other.

"There's obviously been a mistake," said
the lady in the green hat. She pushed Mr
Norm to one side of the stage. "We'll hear
Mr Snorm's poem, if you please," she said
sternly, making sure Mr Norm didn't have
a chance to get to the microphone.

Mr Snorm was very neat and tidy. He had
well-combed hair and clean fingernails. He
looked at Mr Norm with distain, cleared

his throat and read his poem. It was about red sunsets and fairies dancing in a mystical circle, and it had just enough lines to fit neatly onto a greetings card.

It was all too much for Mr Norm. He'd spent weeks preparing to read his poem out loud. He wasn't going to be thwarted now. The moment Mr Snorm finished, he made a lunge for the microphone and grabbed it. There was a bit of a scuffle as the lady in the green hat and the man from the greetings card company tried to take it away from him, but Mr Norm clung on.

Someone at the back of the hall shouted, "Let Mr Norm read his poem!"

Then someone else shouted out, "Yes, we're all sick of fairies and sunsets!"

Then a few other people joined in with "Don't be spoilsports, let him have a go!"

The judges didn't want to look mean, so they had no option but to leave Mr Norm with the microphone.

He cleared his throat and began to read.

He started with the bit about the withered hand crawling about under the bed. A few people in the audience began mumbling, but Mr Norm was blithely unaware of them. He continued with his poem:

"So, little darling, you'd better not sleep tight,
Because there's a vampire on the loose tonight.
There's a scarecrow hiding under the bed,
And a monster that's going to chop off your head."

When he got to the bit about the monster,
the mumblings got louder, and there were
a few squawks of disapproval, but still he
continued.

"There's a lady who's committed a terrible crime.
And something hiding in a bucket of slime.
And in the cupboard, if you dare look,
There's the ghost of your granny hung up on
   a hook."

The bit about the ghost of someone's
granny hung up on a hook was the final
straw. The lady judge in the green hat made
a dive for the microphone and snatched it
away. Shouts went up from the audience.

It seemed everyone had their own opinion about Mr Norm's poem. Some people thought it was repulsive but some thought it was refreshing.

54

What was best of all, what Ben and Mary thought was really good news, was that the two people who had shouted out "fantastic" and "brilliant" were from a famous local rock band called The Dark Ones. They had been getting ready to rehearse in another room when they heard the commotion on stage and came to see what was happening. They heard Mr Norm's poem and thought it was by far the best. They said with some rewriting it might make a great song – just the kind of thing they were looking for.

Mr Norm thanked them and said they could do what they wanted with it. He said he had decided he didn't want to be a poet after all. It was too much trouble.

"I'll do something else instead," he declared.

"Like what?" asked Ben.

Dad said he wasn't sure.

Mrs Norm said she'd had a few ideas about what they could all be doing next. She wasn't prepared to share her ideas though. The only thing she would say was that not only would her ideas please Ben and Mary, but they would also please their favourite teacher, Miss Jones.

Ben and Mary were dubious.

That night, just before bed, Ben asked,
"I wonder what kind of ideas
Mum's had?"

"Silly ones, no doubt,"
replied Mary. "She'll
come up with something
that's bound to embarrass us."

Mary was certainly right about that.

The Impossible Parents Go Green

At school Miss Jones decided to talk to the class about her favourite subject – Saving the Earth.

Miss Jones was tall and thin and kind, and wore a necklace made of wooden beads. They smelled of jasmine but looked like sheeps' droppings. Miss Jones prided herself on being an environmentalist. She worried about saving the planet. She worried about animals and plants being poisoned and about whales having their blow-holes bunged up with babies' dummies and plastic bags. Worrying about the earth was Miss Jones's hobby. You could tell how much Miss Jones worried just by looking at her.

Ben and Mary were impressed by Miss Jones. In the school holidays, they would see her shovelling dead hedgehogs off busy roads with her pooper-scooper. Of course, Miss Jones was right to worry. The world was becoming more and more polluted. Factories and power stations spewed out toxic fumes, and without people like Miss Jones things would be even worse. Still, Ben and Mary couldn't work out how scooping flattened hedgehogs off the roads with a pooper-scooper helped.

That morning Miss Jones was going to talk to the class about how people were responsible for looking after the world and all the animals in it. She held up a picture of a sweet little fox. "Can you imagine who

would wear a coat
made out of this
lovely creature?"
she asked.

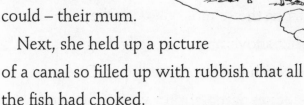

Ben and Mary
could – their mum.

Next, she held up a picture
of a canal so filled up with rubbish that all
the fish had choked.

"Can you imagine what kind of terrible
person would do this?" she asked.

Ben and Mary knew very well – their dad.

They'd seen him throw an old telly into
the canal. Another time they just managed
to stop him throwing half-empty paint tins
and old brushes into the

water. Dad was
an ecological
disaster
all by
himself.

In the past, Ben and Mary had tried to get their parents to change in all sorts of ways. Caring about the environment was one of them. But Mr and Mrs Norm just carried on doing what they liked doing. Mrs Norm

practised her belly-dancing in front of the mirror. Mr Norm practised

being a pop star with his imaginary guitar. And neither of them paid any attention to the environment.

"It'd be easier talking to one of Miss Jones's squashed hedgehogs than to them," said Mary.

"A squashed hedgehog would have more brains," said Ben.

Then, that very afternoon, when Mary and Ben came home from school, something quite remarkable and unexpected happened.

"We're turning green," said Mrs Norm.

"Not physically," said Mr Norm. "That would be horrible. What we mean is we're going to become more eco ... eco ... er..."

"Ecological?" said Ben.

"That's it!" said Mr Norm, who was very bad at pronouncing big words. "After everything you've told us about Miss Jones, we've decided to follow her example and do our bit to save the earth."

"That's exactly what I've been thinking about ever since Dad decided to give up being a poet," said Mum.

This pleased Ben and Mary, but they were also worried. After all, their parents weren't just impossible parents, they were the most impossibly impossible of all impossible parents.

"What exactly do you mean?" asked Mary.

"Well, we are against things like fox hunting and culling badgers," said Mrs Norm.

"Of course we are," said Dad. "Neither of them are as tasty as chickens."

"And we are against killing whales."

"Positively," said Dad. "They probably taste awful with chips."

"I don't think either of you really understands what being green is all about," sighed Mary.

"Of course we do," said Mr Norm.

"Well, we can all start by recycling," said Ben, who was fed up with all the rubbish and bits of junk piling up in the bins at the back of the house.

"*Recycling?* I'm not recycling!" said Mr

Norm. "I did enough cycling in my youth."

Ben and Mary groaned. They thought something was bound to go wrong. And, of course, it did.

The next morning, when Ben and Mary came down for breakfast, their parents were sitting at the table utterly naked.

"Put something on!" screeched Mary.

"That's disgusting!" said Ben.

"We're only being natural, dears," said Mrs Norm, "and nothing could be more natural than being naked."

"Think of all those poor freezing sheep that have the wool stolen off their backs just so we can keep warm," said Dad.

"Naked parents are totally vomit-making," said Ben.

"And they wobble," said Mary. "Naked wobbly parents are the most disgusting of all."

"Well, it *is* a bit chilly," admitted Mrs Norm, and she sent Dad down to the cellar to find some old potato sacks. She cut out holes for their heads and arms and they wriggled into them.

"You're not driving us to school dressed like that," said Ben.

"Drive? We can't possibly drive you to school," said Mrs Norm.

"No, we're getting rid of the car later on this morning," said Dad. "We remembered what you told us about cars polluting the atmosphere with notorious grasses."

"We said obnoxious gasses!" shouted Ben, marching out of the house.

"They're always getting things wrong," sighed Mary. "Remember when Dad's nose dripped all the time …"

"… and his nose-ring got rusty? He had to switch it to the other nostril. That was gross," said Ben. "Remember his nose went septic and he had to have an injection up his nostril? Why can't we have ordinary parents?"

Ben and Mary got another surprise at lunchtime.

Inside their lunch boxes, instead of their usual sandwiches, they found a lump of yak's cheese and bean sprouts.

They dumped the lot. Not even the pigeons would eat it.

Then, after school, they discovered that Mum and Dad had thrown out the telly.

"TV transmissions fry birds' brains," said Dad. "Their brains fall out of their ears and are eaten by worms."

Ben decided Dad's brains had fallen out of his ears years ago. Not only did they miss their favourite soap on TV, but when dinner came it was as bad as the stuff in their lunch boxes. They couldn't even *guess* what it was.

Things were no better at bedtime.

First, Dad insisted on candlelight. He said it took the equivalent of an entire forest just to keep an electric light bulb going for an hour. Ben said not even Miss Jones believed *that*.

Then they found that their duvets had vanished and been replaced by two itchy straw blankets.

"Duvets are not ecological," said Mrs Norm. "They're stuffed with feathers plucked from harmless geese. A naked goose is a heart-rending sight," she said.

"But you two haven't seen any kind of geese for years," said Mary.

"Except those you've cooked," said Ben.

Mary and Ben wished they hadn't mentioned anything about ecology to their parents. They decided they had to get them back to their normal impossible selves before things got *really* bad. They needed a fantastic plan. The trouble was, they couldn't think of one.

At school, Ben and Mary were having a rotten time. Word had got round that Mr and Mrs Norm were wandering the streets wearing nothing but sacks.

And Mary's worst enemy, Alice Frimp, told everyone that she'd seen Mrs Norm collecting worms from the front garden.

Mary said it wasn't true. She said her mum had been planting carrots and sprouts. But of course no one believed her. Everyone was far more interested in the idea of Mrs Norm collecting worms for supper.

"She mixes them up with spaghetti to make dinner bigger," said Alice Frimp. "Sometimes if there's no spaghetti in the house Mrs Norm puts the worms in a very hot pan till they stop wriggling, and then she covers them in tomato sauce."

Mary hated Alice Frimp. She hated her even more than she hated worms. She wished she could change Alice Frimp into a worm.

Mr Norm was also causing embarrassment. A rumour had got round that he'd gone into Mr Azteck's shop to buy some tape to mend the hole in the ozone layer.

Ben and Mary blushed furiously every time someone mentioned something their parents had been up to. Not that you could see them blush. They'd developed pimply red rashes from sleeping under the itchy blankets.

The need to find a plan became even more urgent after Dad's next hare-brained scheme.

One morning they were woken by a terrible rumbling noise from downstairs. The whole house was shaking. At first they thought it was an earthquake and they stood in the door-frame, just like they'd been told to by Miss Jones at school.

They weren't sure exactly where Miss Jones got her information from, but she was full of useful tips on how to survive major disasters. Earthquakes and comets smashing into the earth were just two of her favourite subjects. The head teacher said Miss Jones was a minefield of useful information.

When Mary and Ben realized that they weren't in the middle of an earthquake, they rushed downstairs to see what was happening.

Dad was in the kitchen. Somehow he had got hold of a drill. It wasn't just any old drill. It was the biggest, loudest most fearsome-looking drill imaginable. It was the kind of drill builders used to dig vast holes in the middle of the road. Only Mr Norm wasn't in the middle of a road, was he? He was in the middle of the kitchen, bouncing up and down on the drill like a deranged frog, and there was a hole in the kitchen floor that was already about two foot deep and four foot wide.

The kitchen light flickered on and off. The cups and plates rattled. The pans jangled. The knives and forks clattered in the drawers, and Mary and Ben could hardly see for the dust.

They decided that the yak's yogurt and Peruvian juju berries Dad had been eating had finally driven him mad. They yelled at him to stop but he couldn't hear them above the din. So they gave up and left him to get on with it.

Half an hour later he came into the living-room covered in mud. He said that he'd borrowed the drill from a friend who worked for the council and that he was digging a well so they could all have real water.

"But we've got water in the taps!" said Mary.

"And it's drinkable," said Ben.

"I'm after the kind of water you get from natural springs," said Mr Norm. "The bubbly stuff that tastes like tasteless lemonade."

With that he went back into the kitchen to carry on drilling.

Days passed. Things got worse. Dad gave up digging the well, but only because the neighbours called the council, and the council called the police and the police threatened to arrest him for disturbing the peace. Mum made him fill up the hole.

Unfortunately they were both still determined to carry on being green.

Ben and Mary started to wear pegs on their noses because Mr and Mrs Norm were eating so many soya beans that they couldn't stop passing wind. They sounded like a couple of old trumpets. When Smudge the cat moved into the neighbour's house Mary said it was because Mum was feeding it vegetarian sausages, but Ben was convinced that it was because the cat had a sensitive nose.

By now Mary and Ben were only pretending to eat at home. They scraped the food Mum served them into plastic bags and chucked them in the dustbin when no one was looking. Then they went to their friend Pattie Rotti's house and had secret hamburgers and chips and all the other wonderful stuff that Mrs Norm had stopped cooking.

It was at Pattie Rotti's house that Mary finally worked out a plan for getting their parents back to normal.

When she told Ben the plan, he thought it was fantastic.

The next morning was Saturday and Ben and Mary went off to get the things they needed to put Mary's plan into action.

First, they went to the health food store and bought a gigantic carton of Old Yak Yoghurt. Then they mixed in some crunchy gravel from Pattie Rotti's garden. Then they added a little bit of Smudge's cat litter for extra effect.

Next, they went to the paper shop and bought a bottle of green ink. Then they went to the chemist and bought a green sponge. It was exactly like the green sponge they already had in the bathroom at home.

They already had green towels, so now

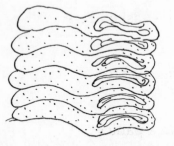

everything in the bathroom would be green.

Finally, they went home and sneaked the green ink and the green sponge up into their bedroom, and put the carton of yak yoghurt in the fridge. Then they were ready to put their plan into action.

"We had a wonderful lesson at school today," they fibbed when they sat down to supper that evening.

"Was it about ecology, dears?" asked Mrs Norm.

"It was more about the *dangers* of too much ecology," said Mary.

"Dangers?" asked Dad, with a panicky look in his eyes. "What kind of dangers?"

"Well, Miss Jones said that sometimes parents who are too environmentally friendly can actually turn green," said Mary.

"Yes," said Ben. "And it's very dangerous. If you do turn green, you have to have all your skin peeled off."

"Just like a banana," said Mary, darkly.

"Rubbish," said Mum.

"Rubbish," said Dad.

But Mum and Dad weren't quite sure whether it was rubbish or not. Their voices sounded a bit squeaky.

Can you imagine Mr and Mrs Norm with their skin peeled off? No wonder they were worried!

Getting Mum and Dad *worried* about turning green and having to be peeled was only the first part of Mary's fantastic plan. The second part was actually getting their skin to *turn* green. She'd worked that out as well. That's why they'd bought the green ink and the sponge.

That night, after their baths, Mary and Ben only pretended to go to sleep. Instead, they

sneaked back into the bathroom. Mary had
the green ink. Ben had the new green sponge.

They poured the green ink onto the new
sponge, then went back to bed, taking with
them the old green sponge that Mr and Mrs
Norm usually used.

Thank goodness their mum and dad had insisted on candlelight, they thought. It suited Mary's plan. The house was so gloomy that you couldn't see anything properly.

After a while they heard Dad splashing about in the bath.

He dried himself on one of the green towels, then he went to bed.

Shortly afterwards Mum did the same.

As soon as Mary and Ben heard Mum
and Dad snoring they sneaked back into
the bathroom and, very carefully so they
wouldn't get any ink over themselves,
cleaned the bath. They put the old green
sponge back where it should be and popped
the inky sponge into a plastic bag to throw
away later. Now no one could have guessed
what had made the bath water turn green.

In the morning, Mary and Ben were woken by horrible screams. Mr and Mrs Norm had discovered they'd turned green. They had absolutely no idea that the green ink had caused it. They decided Miss Jones had been right! Not only was their skin green, but the whites of their eyes and their tongues were as well. They looked like two gigantic cabbages.

"Miss Jones says sometimes you can reverse the process by eating yak yoghurt," said Mary.

"Just like the stuff that's in the fridge," said Ben.

Mr and Mrs Norm dashed to the fridge. They grabbed the yoghurt and gobbled it up wildly, their teeth crunching and grating on the bits of garden grit and cat litter that Ben and Mary had poured into it the day before. It was a horrible sound.

Then there was an even more horrible sound. It was the kind of horrible sound someone makes when they get grit and cat litter caught in a hole in their tooth. Dad roared like an injured bull and leapt around the table clutching his mouth. He'd lost a big filling.

Mary and Ben said he'd have to go to the dentist. But not just any old dentist. He'd have to go to a dentist who practised Natural Dentistry. Natural dentists were especially for environmentalists, they explained.

"First they scrape your teeth with pebbles. Then they saw through them with a hacksaw," said Mary. "That's only after they've sanded them down and drilled them with a hand drill," said Ben.

"It's all very natural," said Mary. "You'll love it."

Ben and Mary were making all of this up of course, but Dad didn't know. The fear of having to have his skin peeled off *and* having his teeth sawn with a hacksaw was too much for him. He said

he refused to have
Natural Dentistry.
What's more, he
wasn't going to let
anyone peel Mrs

Norm's skin off either. He said he liked her
skin where it was. On Mrs Norm.

"I'm going back to being normal," he said.

Mrs Norm agreed. She said she wasn't
going to wear stupid sacks
any more. She marched
upstairs and fluffed
up the duvets and
threw out the itchy
straw blankets.

In time, the
green ink wore off.
Mum went back to
wearing her fishnet
body stocking and her
pink feather boa, and

Dad's tooth stopped aching. He dumped all the yak yoghurt and sprouting beans. He started wearing his ordinary clothes again and was soon devouring vast quantities of beefburgers and chips.

Mary's fantastic plan had worked! Mum and Dad were back to being their normal impossible selves, although they *were* a little bit better about things like recycling.

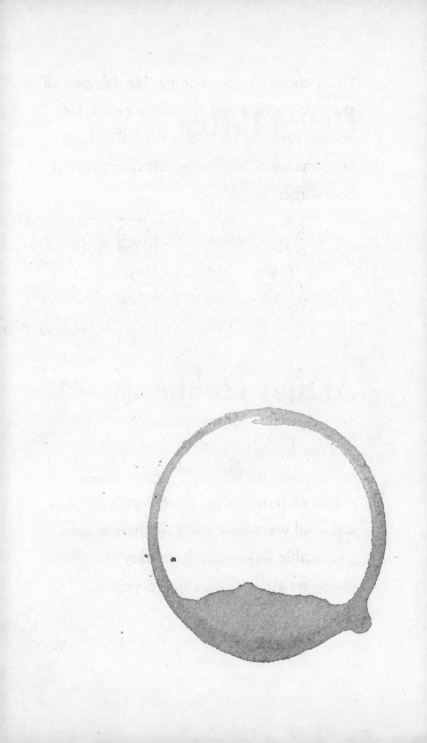

Brian Patten is a famous poet. The stuff he writes for adults is mostly sad and the stuff he writes for children is mostly funny. Over the years he's noticed how children always think their own parents are the most embarrassing parents in the entire world. They are usually right.

Arthur Robins did the drawings. He works with inks and paints, and gets more on himself than on the paper, so he wears scruffy old jumpers, paint-splattered trousers, slippers and a woolly hat in winter. He doesn't have a nose-ring but sometimes has a beard, the look he thinks is called … embarrassing.